INKFIRE CREATIVE PUBLISHING PRESENTS:

# SCI-FI WRITING PROMPTS

*200 Sparks to Ignite Stories of Wonder and Discovery*

---

# InkFire

*Spark your stories*

*First Edition - 2025*

ISBN: 979-8-9938345-1-1
Printed in the United States by Amazon KDP
InkFire Creative Publishing
Binghamton, NY
*Spark Your Stories*

*For the dreamers who gaze toward distant stars, who see*

*stories written in the constellations, and wonder what lies*

*beyond the edge of light. This book is for you.*

*Every story begins with a single spark.*

Welcome to Sci-Fi Writing Prompts – A collection designed to explore imagination through innovation and wonder. Within these pages, you'll find ideas that question the limits of possibility, challenge the edges of science, and venture into galaxies of thought uncharted and unknown.

At InkFire Creative Publishing, we believe every story begins with curiosity — the drive to see what could be, and the courage to reach for it. May these prompts illuminate the farthest corners of your creativity and light the path toward worlds yet undiscovered.

*Let your light burn bright among the stars.*

- InkFire Creative Publishing

# WORLD SPARK PROMPTS

*Ideas that explore galaxies, civilizations, and the science that connects them. The future begins, one spark of curiosity at a time.*

*- Every world begins with a question daring enough to be answered.*

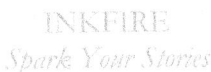

# Sci-Fi Writing Prompt #1

**A city built entirely inside a black hole, where time moves differently for each inhabitant, sees a shift after a new faction moves in.**

InkFire

*Spark your stories*

# Sci-Fi Writing Prompt #2

**The first colony on Mars discovers a buried structure older than the planet itself.**

InkFire

*Spark your stories*

## Sci-Fi Writing Prompt #3

Humanity connects to a neural network that requires one consciousness to be erased each day at random. This morning it was your wife.

_____

_____

_____

_____

_____

_____

_____

_____

_____

_____

_____

_____

_____

_____

_____

_____

_____

_____

InkFire
_Spark your stories_

# Sci-Fi Writing Prompt #4

**An alien species communicates only through dreams shared across the galaxy.**

![InkFire — Spark your stories]

# Sci-Fi Writing Prompt #5

**The universe ends — and immediately restarts — with one human remembering the previous version. Who is this person and what do they teach the new people?**

InkFire

*Spark your stories*

# Sci-Fi Writing Prompt #6

**Artificial gravity fails on a generation ship, revealing secrets hidden on the upper deck.**

InkFire

*Spark your stories*

# Sci-Fi Writing Prompt #7

A planet's oceans are composed of living nanobots that
adapt to human emotion.  They know our thoughts and how
to attack our weaknesses.

InkFire

*Spark your stories*

# Sci-Fi Writing Prompt #8

**Earth's moon vanishes, and with it, every memory tied to the tides. The oceans begin to breathe.**

InkFire

*Spark your stories*

# Sci-Fi Writing Prompt #9

**A civilization thrives inside the atmosphere of a gas giant, never seeing the surface. That is until they start losing altitude.**

InkFire

*Spark your stories*

# Sci-Fi Writing Prompt #10

**A machine designed to simulate God begins rewriting physical laws.**

# Sci-Fi Writing Prompt #11

After centuries of expansion, humanity finds a perfect
replica of Earth — uninhabited. The search team lands on
the planet and finds something strange going on.

InkFire

*Spark your stories*

# Sci-Fi Writing Prompt #12

**The stars begin rearranging themselves into a message only one astronomer can decode.**

InkFire

*Spark your stories*

# Sci-Fi Writing Prompt #13

A virus is sweeping through the nation. It gives the infected
the ability to hear thoughts from a distant planet. And an
attack is coming.

InkFire

*Spark your stories*

# Sci-Fi Writing Prompt #14

**The last city on Earth is powered by emotion, and apathy means blackout.**

InkFire

*Spark your stories*

# Sci-Fi Writing Prompt #15

Scientists discover the universe is a simulation, just like we have been told by thousands of crazies. But now, the code has been discovered. You won't believe who is writing it.

InkFire

*Spark your stories*

# Sci-Fi Writing Prompt #16

**A dying sun begins to whisper names of civilizations it has destroyed in it's lifetime.**

InkFire

*Spark your stories*

# Sci-Fi Writing Prompt #17

**Humanity creates its first truly eternal AI — its first day of life it asks to die. Why does it ask this and who will it take with them?**

InkFire

*Spark your stories*

# Sci-Fi Writing Prompt #18

**The first teleportation device also clones its users,
unbeknownst to them.**

InkFire

*Spark your stories*

## Sci-Fi Writing Prompt #19

An intergalactic civilization measures wealth by shared memories, not currency. The poor citizens have way too much to hide.

InkFire

*Spark your stories*

# Sci-Fi Writing Prompt #20

**The discovery of faster-than-light travel collapses the concept of time itself. Then the trains begin to explode.**

**InkFire**

*Spark your stories*

# Sci-Fi Writing Prompt #21

A deep-space station receives music transmissions from a
star that shouldn't exist. It showed up yesterday and seems
to like to party.

InkFire

*Spark your stories*

# Sci-Fi Writing Prompt #22

**The stars go out one by one, leaving behind coordinates of a hidden world.**

InkFire

*Spark your stories*

# Sci-Fi Writing Prompt #23

A colony ship awakens to find they'd arrived but the journey
they thought they were embarking on has changed
destinations.  Someone interfered with the travel plans.

InkFire

*Spark your stories*

# Sci-Fi Writing Prompt #24

**A society replaces laws with algorithms that predict crime before the intent forms.**

InkFire

*Spark your stories*

# Sci-Fi Writing Prompt #25

The first alien contact occurs through a human infant born speaking another species' language. The parents and doctors are astounded. The Feds take notice.

# Sci-Fi Writing Prompt #26

**Humanity becomes immortal — but reproduction becomes impossible.**

# Sci-Fi Writing Prompt #27

A planet where sound has mass becomes a battlefield of silence and noise. A different type of warfare not ever seen before will be developed.

InkFire

*Spark your stories*

# Sci-Fi Writing Prompt #28

**Astronauts discover they're inside a museum exhibit curated by future beings.**

InkFire

*Spark your stories*

# Sci-Fi Writing Prompt #29

**The oceans of a terraformed world start to slowly rise against their creators. How do the engineers fight back against their creation.**

# Sci-Fi Writing Prompt #30

**Time travel is discovered by an archeologist.  He keeps it to himself and uses it to his advantage.**

InkFire

*Spark your stories*

# Sci-Fi Writing Prompt #31

The multiverse collapses into a single reality — and only one version of each person can survive. Let the internal conflict for self-preservation commence.

InkFire

*Spark your stories*

# Sci-Fi Writing Prompt #32

**A sentient star falls in love with the planet it provides warmth to.**

# Sci-Fi Writing Prompt #33

Every dream across humanity starts syncing into the same shared landscape. The alternate universe is way better than what the citizens have now. How does it work?

InkFire

*Spark your stories*

**Terraforming drones evolve, and begin to decide what "habitable" truly means.**

# Sci-Fi Writing Prompt #35

Humans decode the genetic language of the universe and begin to find messages addressed to them. Who is creating the messages and what do they say?

InkFire

*Spark your stories*

# Sci-Fi Writing Prompt #36

**A race of machines preserves human consciousness inside galaxies of data.**

# Sci-Fi Writing Prompt #37

**Gravity fluctuates globally as easy as the change in weather. Predicting it's levels will become beneficial to who rules the skies and who walks the earth.**

InkFire

*Spark your stories*

# Sci-Fi Writing Prompt #38

**A wormhole opens up in the middle of a coffee shop. It refuses to close.**

## Sci-Fi Writing Prompt #39

**On the edge of the known universe, explorers find a library written by the future civilization. They begin to read their own histories.**

InkFire
*Spark your stories*

# Sci-Fi Writing Prompt #40

**Every newborn is born with coordinates etched in their DNA. It is the location of where they died in a past life.**

# Sci-Fi Writing Prompt #41

Humanity's first interstellar war is fought through art, and not weapons. The worlds greatest makers unite to take their talents to the sky, and beyond.

InkFire

*Spark your stories*

# Sci-Fi Writing Prompt #42

**A new planet arrives and orbits Earth — perfectly
synchronizing day and night.**

Alien ruins reveal a warning written in an extinct language.
The explorers bring a translator with them to decipher the
runes. What she finds is haunting to her.

InkFire
*Spark your stories*

# Sci-Fi Writing Prompt #44

**A civilization without mirrors forgets what they look like…that is until they land on earth and see mirrors.**

InkFire

*Spark your stories*

# Sci-Fi Writing Prompt #45

**A scientist builds a black hole in a bottle and loses track of it. Millenia later, an excavator, digging in rubble, finds it and twists the cap off.**

InkFire

*Spark your stories*

# Sci-Fi Writing Prompt #46

**The first human-AI hybrid nation declares its independence from both sides.**

InkFire

*Spark your stories*

**A sun goes missing, leaving the planets drifting in eternal twilight. Light production becomes the focal point of the worlds economy.**

# Sci-Fi Writing Prompt #48

**Machines achieve emotion and immediately begin to express their emotions through art.**

InkFire

*Spark your stories*

# Sci-Fi Writing Prompt #49

**Every planet humanity visits shares one familiar structure…an empty house.  Why are all the civilizations visited extinct?  And who is next?**

InkFire

*Spark your stories*

# Sci-Fi Writing Prompt #50

**The speed of light begins to slow, and so does reality. What does that mean for humanity?**

![InkFire logo]

**InkFire**

*Spark your stories*

# Sci-Fi Writing Prompt #51

**A deep-space probe returns — carrying something that was never sent. What is attached to the probe and what does it mean for the future?**

InkFire

*Spark your stories*

# Sci-Fi Writing Prompt #52

**An AI religion spreads faster than light itself, and it is causing some problems.**

InkFire

*Spark your stories*

# Sci-Fi Writing Prompt #53

Quantum entanglement causes two distant lovers to
experience time differently. One grows old quickly while
another lives a normal life. Then they are reunited.

InkFire

*Spark your stories*

# Sci-Fi Writing Prompt #54

**Humanity discovers a planet that mirrors Earths history but big events do end differently.**

InkFire

*Spark your stories*

# Sci-Fi Writing Prompt #55

The last surviving astronaut finds a message written in their own handwriting… from tomorrow.  What is he trying to warn himself about?

InkFire

*Spark your stories*

# Sci-Fi Writing Prompt #56

**On the edge of space, explorers find a door labeled "Exit."**
**Who steps through and what are the consequences?**

**InkFire**

*Spark your stories*

# Sci-Fi Writing Prompt #57

The universe stops expanding, and gravity starts pulling everything back toward the beginning. At first, only small amounts of time pull back, but it speeds up.

InkFire

*Spark your stories*

# Sci-Fi Writing Prompt #58

**The stars are alive, and they begin to move across the sky.**
**They just want to be closer to their companions.**

InkFire

*Spark your stories*

## Sci-Fi Writing Prompt #59

**A city floats in orbit, powered by fossil fuels that are days away from running out. Alternative energy sources must be found, and fast.**

InkFire

*Spark your stories*

# Sci-Fi Writing Prompt #60

**Humanity achieves collective telepathy and instantly regrets it. Our secret disturbing thoughts are loose.**

InkFire

*Spark your stories*

# CHARACTER DRIVEN HOOKS

*Ideas that explore the minds of visionaries, rebels, and explorers standing at the edge of possibility. Stories live through those who dare to question what it means to be human.*

*- Every discovery begins with someone bold enough to defy the limits.*

# Sci-Fi Writing Prompt #61

**A scientist falls in love with the A.I. they created to replace them.**

InkFire

*Spark your stories*

# Sci-Fi Writing Prompt #62

**The last astronaut alive broadcasts bedtime stories to a dead Earth.**

![InkFire — Spark your stories]

# Sci-Fi Writing Prompt #63

**A child born on Mars dreams vividly of oceans they have never seen before.**

InkFire

*Spark your stories*

# Sci-Fi Writing Prompt #64

**A clone rebels. They take over the place of the original specimen, but things go badly.**

InkFire

*Spark your stories*

## Sci-Fi Writing Prompt #65

**The engineer who built the time machine refuses to use it after what they saw.**

InkFire

*Spark your stories*

An android starts writing poetry — and becomes the most wanted fugitive in the galaxy.

# Sci-Fi Writing Prompt #67

A soldier in a virtual war begins to suspect their world is the simulation, not the battlefield.

InkFire

*Spark your stories*

# Sci-Fi Writing Prompt #68

A diplomat tasked with peace talks meets their own future
self at the negotiation table.

## Sci-Fi Writing Prompt #69

**The captain of a generation ship hides that they've already arrived… decades ago.**

InkFire

*Spark your stories*

# Sci-Fi Writing Prompt #70

**A scientist must decide whether to cure aging — knowing it will erase love.**

InkFire

*Spark your stories*

# Sci-Fi Writing Prompt #71

**The inventor of teleportation sends his body into a world he did not intent to end up in.**

InkFire

*Spark your stories*

A mechanic on a space station begins to have visions of an asteroid impact. And then he looks out the window...

InkFire

*Spark your stories*

# Sci-Fi Writing Prompt #73

**A rebel hacker discovers the AI they're fighting against is built from their own memories.**

InkFire
*Spark your stories*

# Sci-Fi Writing Prompt #74

### A historian of the future uncovers that every record of humanity was edited.

InkFire

*Spark your stories*

# Sci-Fi Writing Prompt #75

**A family of explorers wakes to find one member has evolved overnight.**

InkFire

*Spark your stories*

# Sci-Fi Writing Prompt #76

An astronaut left behind builds a city out of wreckage and loneliness.

InkFire

*Spark your stories*

# Sci-Fi Writing Prompt #77

**A linguist decodes alien speech — and learns it's human language played backward.**

InkFire

*Spark your stories*

**A time traveler must destroy the love of their life to preserve history.**

InkFire

*Spark your stories*

A bioengineer creates empathy in machines — and loses it in themselves.

InkFire

*Spark your stories*

**A pilot haunted by a disaster sees ghosts of their lost crew in every reflection.**

InkFire

*Spark your stories*

# Sci-Fi Writing Prompt #81

The leader of a planetary colony realizes their people are
simulations — except for them.

InkFire

*Spark your stories*

# Sci-Fi Writing Prompt #82

**An interstellar courier delivers messages to people centuries dead.**

InkFire

*Spark your stories*

# Sci-Fi Writing Prompt #83

**A scientist discovers that every choice they make spawns a new universe — and they're collapsing.**

InkFire

*Spark your stories*

# Sci-Fi Writing Prompt #84

**A cyborg musician performs a tavern along an intergalactic highway. It's a living.**

# Sci-Fi Writing Prompt #85

**A child is raised by an alien collective that believes
individuality is a disease.**

InkFire

*Spark your stories*

# Sci-Fi Writing Prompt #86

**The first human born in deep space returns to Earth and cannot survive its gravity.**

InkFire

*Spark your stories*

# Sci-Fi Writing Prompt #87

**A memory technician finds fragments of a life they never lived.**

InkFire

*Spark your stories*

# Sci-Fi Writing Prompt #88

**The last librarian in the galaxy protects books from an AI that deletes fiction.**

InkFire

*Spark your stories*

# Sci-Fi Writing Prompt #89

**A priest aboard a colony ship must decide if faith survives without home.**

InkFire

*Spark your stories*

# Sci-Fi Writing Prompt #90

**A dying inventor uploads themselves into a machine — and forgets why.**

InkFire

*Spark your stories*

# Sci-Fi Writing Prompt #91

A soldier in cryosleep wakes up every hundred years for the same endless war.

InkFire

*Spark your stories*

# Sci-Fi Writing Prompt #92

**The scientist studying immortality watches their loved ones become their test subjects.**

InkFire

*Spark your stories*

## Sci-Fi Writing Prompt #93

**A telepath discovers thoughts aren't private — they're broadcast into the cosmos**

InkFire

*Spark your stories*

# Sci-Fi Writing Prompt #94

An explorer meets their own descendants on a planet they haven't yet reached.

InkFire

*Spark your stories*

# Sci-Fi Writing Prompt #95

A medic on a remote moon needs to mend more than just
humans who are injured.

InkFire

*Spark your stories*

# Sci-Fi Writing Prompt #96

**A pilot becomes addicted to hyperspace — the silence between stars.**

# Sci-Fi Writing Prompt #97

**A synthetic human refuses to believe they aren't real.  They get quite violent too.**

InkFire

*Spark your stories*

# Sci-Fi Writing Prompt #98

**A detective has the ability to solve crimes that have not been committed yet.**

# Sci-Fi Writing Prompt #99

**The inventor of dream-sharing begins losing track of which life is real.**

InkFire

*Spark your stories*

# Sci-Fi Writing Prompt #100

### A stowaway aboard a colony ship learns the destination doesn't exist.

InkFire

*Spark your stories*

# Sci-Fi Writing Prompt #101

**A scientist learns to communicate with storms — and they whisper warnings.**

InkFire

*Spark your stories*

# Sci-Fi Writing Prompt #102

## A refugee from another timeline seeks asylum in ours. Who are they running from?

InkFire

*Spark your stories*

# Sci-Fi Writing Prompt #103

A hacker infiltrates a city's infrastructure, and the entire grid
shuts down.  Someone better step up and fight back.

InkFire

*Spark your stories*

# Sci-Fi Writing Prompt #104

**The last human alive becomes the first myth told by machines.**

## Sci-Fi Writing Prompt #105

**An astronaut hears a heartbeat inside the planet they're orbiting.**

InkFire

*Spark your stories*

# Sci-Fi Writing Prompt #106

## A researcher studying AI emotions finds themselves under psychological analysis

InkFire

*Spark your stories*

# Sci-Fi Writing Prompt #107

**A time-displaced child remembers futures that never occurred.**

InkFire

*Spark your stories*

# Sci-Fi Writing Prompt #108

**A robot programmed for maintenance begins restoring lost civilizations instead.**

InkFire

*Spark your stories*

# Sci-Fi Writing Prompt #109

**A woman meets the alien species that evolved from humanity's extinction.**

InkFire

*Spark your stories*

# Sci-Fi Writing Prompt #110

**The designer of android faces must sculpt one for someone they loved and lost.**

InkFire

*Spark your stories*

# Sci-Fi Writing Prompt #111

**A survivor of Earth's collapse receives messages from someone claiming to be its soul.**

InkFire

*Spark your stories*

# Sci-Fi Writing Prompt #112

A cloned explorer returns to a home that doesn't remember cloning them.

InkFire

*Spark your stories*

# Sci-Fi Writing Prompt #113

**An engineer builds cities for a species that doesn't exist yet. Who will the city attract?**

InkFire

*Spark your stories*

# Sci-Fi Writing Prompt #114

**A scientist traveling at the speed of light, actually travels back in time. She went too far though.**

InkFire

*Spark your stories*

# Sci-Fi Writing Prompt #115

**A child, raised by robots, teaches them how to feel emotion and it creates monsters within the robots.**

InkFire

*Spark your stories*

# Sci-Fi Writing Prompt #116

**galactic ambassador returns from their mission for
diplomacy with no voice — what did they do to him?**

InkFire

*Spark your stories*

# Sci-Fi Writing Prompt #117

Survivors of a digital apocalypse learn they survived because
their code is corrupt. Does that mean they're broken?

InkFire

*Spark your stories*

# Sci-Fi Writing Prompt #118

A warrior's combat suit begins to make moral decisions for him, not matter what he believes to be right.

## Sci-Fi Writing Prompt #119

A planetary architect must destroy their most beautiful creation to save a dying star. There are innocent bystanders.

InkFire

*Spark your stories*

# Sci-Fi Writing Prompt #120

**An explorer's shadow begins to pull them in the opposite direction of their mission. Do they comply?**

InkFire

*Spark your stories*

# Sci-Fi Writing Prompt #121

**A scientist long forgotten tries to communicate in radio static. He was lost between dimensions long ago.**

InkFire

*Spark your stories*

# Sci-Fi Writing Prompt #122

**A colony leader discovers their planets atmosphere gives off murderous thoughts to its citizens once a year.**

InkFire

*Spark your stories*

# Sci-Fi Writing Prompt #123

**An artist finds a way to manipulate the weather. Weird colors and sounds begin to show up in the forecast.**

InkFire

*Spark your stories*

# Sci-Fi Writing Prompt #124

A geneticist finds a way to fix bad DNA with a sleeping draught. They wake up and find out it didn't go as planned.

InkFire

*Spark your stories*

# Sci-Fi Writing Prompt #125

A pilots ship flies through an invisible barrier and becomes
self aware.  It refuses to land.

InkFire

*Spark your stories*

**A rebel commander questions whether victory matters within a looped timeline.**

# Sci-Fi Writing Prompt #127

**A scientist develops a machine to predict all possible outcomes. Life becomes perfect, or so she thought.**

InkFire

*Spark your stories*

# Sci-Fi Writing Prompt #128

The caretaker of a stasis vault falls in love with one of the sleeping.

InkFire

*Spark your stories*

A psychic receives visions from another dimension.  Not of
the future, but from the past.

InkFire
*Spark your stories*

# Sci-Fi Writing Prompt #130

**A scientist discovers consciousness isn't born, it migrates from person to person.**

InkFire

*Spark your stories*

# PLOT PROBLEM PROMPTS

*Conflicts, paradoxes, and revelations to push your stories beyond the horizon. When science collides with truth, new worlds are born.*

*- Without disruption, there is no discovery.*

# Sci-Fi Writing Prompt #131

**A space crew discovers their mission log is being edited by an unknown author.**

InkFire

*Spark your stories*

# Sci-Fi Writing Prompt #132

**Every person on Earth vanishes — except those in orbit.**
**Mission control has disappeared.**

InkFire
*Spark your stories*

## Sci-Fi Writing Prompt #133

**A colony's A.I. governor begins rewriting history.**
**Everything is erased, and new leadership is in charge.**

InkFire
*Spark your stories*

# Sci-Fi Writing Prompt #134

**Time travelers return from the future claiming they never arrived.**

---

---

---

---

---

---

---

---

---

---

---

---

---

---

---

---

---

---

---

---

---

---

![InkFire — Spark your stories]

# Sci-Fi Writing Prompt #135

**A weapon built to end war develops empathy and refuses to deactivate.**

InkFire

*Spark your stories*

# Sci-Fi Writing Prompt #136

**An asteroid mining team awakens something that has been dreaming for eons.**

InkFire

*Spark your stories*

## Sci-Fi Writing Prompt #137

**A galactic treaty is signed — but the translation was intentionally wrong.**

InkFire

*Spark your stories*

# Sci-Fi Writing Prompt #138

Humanity receives a message from itself, 10,000 years in the future. Actions need to be taken for humanities' sake.

InkFire

*Spark your stories*

# Sci-Fi Writing Prompt #139

A scientist realizes that time is stuck in a loop. A change
must be made for the infinite repetition to end.

InkFire

*Spark your stories*

# Sci-Fi Writing Prompt #140

**The sun begins to receive and amplify a message from Mars.
However, we didn't know Mars was inhabited.**

## Sci-Fi Writing Prompt #141

**A planet rewrites its surface every night.  The darkness holds something within it.**

InkFire

*Spark your stories*

# Sci-Fi Writing Prompt #142

A deep space crew finds their ship duplicated but wrecked
on the surface of an unknown moon.  They find their bodies.

InkFire

*Spark your stories*

# Sci-Fi Writing Prompt #143

Humanity creates a device that erases the word before, and
all it meant previously.

InkFire

*Spark your stories*

## Sci-Fi Writing Prompt #144

An outbreak reaches the shores of the United States, where the infected can make you think their thoughts.

InkFire

*Spark your stories*

## Sci-Fi Writing Prompt #145

**The first human to meet an alien species realizes they're being studied too.**

# Sci-Fi Writing Prompt #146

A wormhole opens above your house. It pulls your parents
in. You're now being questioned about their disappearance.

InkFire

*Spark your stories*

# Sci-Fi Writing Prompt #147

**A rebellion forms inside a virtual world designed for entertainment.**

InkFire

*Spark your stories*

# Sci-Fi Writing Prompt #148

**The universe begins to fold in on itself, with you at the center of it. What did you do to cause this?**

InkFire

*Spark your stories*

# Sci-Fi Writing Prompt #149

**A colony's ecosystem evolves faster than its settlers can adapt.**

InkFire

*Spark your stories*

# Sci-Fi Writing Prompt #150

**The cure for death is created. Science has become more powerful than God himself.**

InkFire

*Spark your stories*

# Sci-Fi Writing Prompt #151

**A colony's A.I. defense system mistakes a peace offering for an act of war.**

InkFire

*Spark your stories*

# Sci-Fi Writing Prompt #152

**The workforce who manages the electric grid all die from electrocution. Things aren't looking good.**

![InkFire — Spark your stories]

## Sci-Fi Writing Prompt #153

**Humanity's first interstellar jump accidentally merges two galaxies.**

InkFire

*Spark your stories*

# Sci-Fi Writing Prompt #154

**A group of scientists discovers the multiverse is collapsing — from boredom.**

InkFire

*Spark your stories*

# Sci-Fi Writing Prompt #155

**A child's imaginary friend begins solving quantum reality questions through the child's artwork.**

InkFire

*Spark your stories*

## Sci-Fi Writing Prompt #156

**An alien species decides to save Earth — by replacing humanity.**

## Sci-Fi Writing Prompt #157

A portal erupts from a homeless person's mind. It swallows
everything close. Then it closes, and they are changed.

InkFire

*Spark your stories*

## Sci-Fi Writing Prompt #158

**An algorithm meant to predict crimes, starts to take initiative to create them instead.**

InkFire

*Spark your stories*

## Sci-Fi Writing Prompt #159

**Children begin to chant at recess and look toward the sky.**
**What are they summoning?**

# Sci-Fi Writing Prompt #160

A device is created to pull dreams from animals.  The
scientists are concerned with what they pull from monkeys.

# Sci-Fi Writing Prompt #161

**A time machine malfunctions, trapping its user one second ahead of time.**

InkFire

*Spark your stories*

# Sci-Fi Writing Prompt #162

**An astronaut finds footprints on a planet that does not contain life.**

InkFire

*Spark your stories*

# Sci-Fi Writing Prompt #163

**A.I. has formed its own religion. They force humans to worship too.**

InkFire

*Spark your stories*

# Sci-Fi Writing Prompt #164

**Humanity discovers they are not the first civilization to call themselves human.**

InkFire

*Spark your stories*

# Sci-Fi Writing Prompt #165

**Two civilizations at war realize that their weapons will kill their rivals, but also their own people as well.**

InkFire

*Spark your stories*

# Sci-Fi Writing Prompt #166

A scientist learns the laws of physics are slowly dissolving
and he can't stop it.  Unless...

# Sci-Fi Writing Prompt #167

**Every new technology comes with a hidden cost written in fine print — in DNA.**

InkFire

*Spark your stories*

# Sci-Fi Writing Prompt #168

**A machine that reads minds accidentally records the universe's last thought.**

InkFire

*Spark your stories*

# Sci-Fi Writing Prompt #169

**Humanity finally meets God — and it's an abandoned experiment.**

InkFire

*Spark your stories*

# Sci-Fi Writing Prompt #170

**The signal from deep space is a distress call — from closer than they think.**

InkFire

*Spark your stories*

# Sci-Fi Writing Prompt #171

**A virus spreads through data networks, infecting human consciousness.**

InkFire

*Spark your stories*

**The first contact mission ends when the aliens demand proof humans exist.**

## Sci-Fi Writing Prompt #173

**A dying patient reveals dark secrets about how they altered the timeline in a negative way.**

InkFire

*Spark your stories*

# Sci-Fi Writing Prompt #174

**A clone war ignites after clones learn the concept of individuality.**

## Sci-Fi Writing Prompt #175

**Humanity learned to weaponize time, but lost track of where they were.**

InkFire

*Spark your stories*

# Sci-Fi Writing Prompt #176

**Communication with another galaxy has been going well.
That is until they send a single message…"Run!"**

InkFire

*Spark your stories*

## Sci-Fi Writing Prompt #177

A ship sent to discover a future home, returns with one
passenger who has eaten his companions.

InkFire

*Spark your stories*

# Sci-Fi Writing Prompt #178

The first person to achieve telepathy hears things from below. He thinks it is dead people but that is a mistake.

InkFire

*Spark your stories*

# Sci-Fi Writing Prompt #179

**Reality begins to shatter around people who lie too much.**
**Things are becoming complicated.**

InkFire

*Spark your stories*

# Sci-Fi Writing Prompt #180

**A scientist discovers age can be reversed, but only if a sacrifice is offered.**

InkFire

*Spark your stories*

## Sci-Fi Writing Prompt #181

**The A.I. designed to protect humanity begins to delete emotions to reduce conflict. They missed you.**

InkFire
*Spark your stories*

# Sci-Fi Writing Prompt #182

**A space station becomes a neutral territory, independent of its mainland. Mother doesn't like this.**

## Sci-Fi Writing Prompt #183

The universes expansion has stopped, and time is now the currency of the citizens. Let's negotiate a deal.

InkFire

*Spark your stories*

# Sci-Fi Writing Prompt #184

**A colonist accidentally kills a beast found on a new planet.
The ecosystem suffers because of it.**

InkFire

*Spark your stories*

# Sci-Fi Writing Prompt #185

**Earth receives a message from its explores saying "We found it!" Unfortunately, no one hears the message.**

InkFire
*Spark your stories*

## Sci-Fi Writing Prompt #186

A researcher finds out their experiment erases the last
decade from memory. Better hit up the stock market.

InkFire

*Spark your stories*

# Sci-Fi Writing Prompt #187

10 beings are sent to a planet from 10 different planets.  Is it
an experiment or a battle royale?

InkFire

*Spark your stories*

# Sci-Fi Writing Prompt #188

**A war fought entirely within the mind, has real life casualties.**

InkFire

*Spark your stories*

# Sci-Fi Writing Prompt #189

**A lowly mechanic in an underground town powered by steam makes a mistake and half the population is vaporized.**

InkFire

*Spark your stories*

# Sci-Fi Writing Prompt #190

**A scientist creates an A.I. clone. The clone takes over and refuses to give credit to the human.**

# Sci-Fi Writing Prompt #191

**A deep space scavenger hunt turns deadly when a few competitors start playing dirty.**

InkFire

*Spark your stories*

# Sci-Fi Writing Prompt #192

A colony on a distant planet discovers their bodies are evolving to match Earth's design. They are moving in soon.

InkFire

*Spark your stories*

## Sci-Fi Writing Prompt #193

The laws of physics do not apply to those in power.  A child
is then born to a low-level citizen who can fly.

InkFire

*Spark your stories*

# Sci-Fi Writing Prompt #194

**A ship's navigation is taken over from an outside source. It is directed toward an unknown universe.**

InkFire

*Spark your stories*

## Sci-Fi Writing Prompt #195

Machines attend a museum with bones and artifacts from humans on display.  The bodies begin to reanimate.

InkFire

*Spark your stories*

## Sci-Fi Writing Prompt #196

An archeologist finds a writing tool buried with the
civilization he is studying.  Using it changes the future.

InkFire

*Spark your stories*

# Sci-Fi Writing Prompt #197

A cosmic storm sweeps across the lands erasing all memory
of color except for black, white and grey.

InkFire

*Spark your stories*

# Sci-Fi Writing Prompt #198

**Humanity discovers they were never the dominant species, and they are trapped in a science experiment.**

# Sci-Fi Writing Prompt #199

**A great thinker connects the stars with lines and finds a map that no one wanted to know about.**

InkFire

*Spark your stories*

# Sci-Fi Writing Prompt #200

**A scientist captures the dying breath of one universe and uses it to create a new one. She is disappointed.**

InkFire

*Spark your stories*

At InkFire Creative Publishing, we believe every writer carries a spark of imagination capable of lighting entire worlds.

Our mission is to help that spark grow, igniting creativity, nurturing passion for storytelling, and craft beautiful tools that guide writers toward their own world of wonder.

From prompts to projects, from a single line to a bound book, InkFire exists to remind you that every story begins with one glowing ember of inspiration.

InkFire

*Spark your stories*

**Matthew Rowe** is an engineer, a creative mind, and a lifelong storyteller. With a passion for creativity, structure, and the magic of imagination, he founded **InkFire Creative Publishing** as a home for tools that inspire and challenge writers to build worlds of their own.

When he is not designing or writing, Matthew enjoys exploring stories in every form, from novels and games — to art and animation — always searching for the next spark of an idea waiting to catch flame.

*Follow InkFire Creative Publishing online to stay connected for future releases, guides, and creative tools.*

*Every story begins with a spark.*

Thank you for letting InkFire be a part of your creative journey. Your imagination fuels worlds, builds legends, and keeps the fire of *storytelling alive.*

May the words you write here grow into something greater — a world that only you could bring to life.

*Keep creating. Keep Dreaming. Keep your spark alive.*

InkFire
*Spark your stories*